HUNTER S. THOMPSON

SCREW-JACK

Simon & Schuster
Paperbacks

New York
London
Toronto
Sydney
New Delhi

Simon & Schuster Paperbacks
An Imprint of Simon & Schuster, Inc.
1230 Avenue of the Americas
New York, NY 10020

This Simon & Schuster trade paperback edition July 2023

SIMON & SCHUSTER PAPERBACKS and colophon are
trademarks of Simon & Schuster, Inc.

For information about special discounts for bulk purchases,
please contact Simon & Schuster Special Sales at 1-866-506-1949
or business@simonandschuster.com.

The Simon & Schuster Speakers Bureau can bring authors to your
live event. For more information or to book an event, contact the
Simon & Schuster Speakers Bureau at 1-866-248-3049 or
visit our website at www.simonspeakers.com.

Manufactured in the United States of America

3 5 7 9 10 8 6 4 2

Library of Congress Control Number 00061251

ISBN 978-1-6680-2293-1

TO MONA
for making this outburst possible

CONTENTS

CONTENTS

INTRODUCTION

BY LARS ULRICH

While Hunter S. Thompson's observations and reflections on . . . well, just about everything in his path, have always seemed abstract, a little precocious and—dare I say it—nutty, I challenge anyone to argue that his writings and points of view are not as relevant as ever in today's turbulent seas of social chaos and contradictions.

This collection of delightfully devious and daring short stories (available for public consumption having lived as a private print for a few decades) are missives from Thompson's late-sixties experiences, with each taking us further into his various psyches. There's humor, there's madness, there's craziness and sadness—all qualities of Hunter's that have always swirled around in his head. And these three stories? They're raw, unchecked, yet brimming with potent reflections and analysis of both himself, and of you and me.

Hunter was more than a writer; he was also a philosopher. Just like the big guns, your Kants,

Nietzsches, and Sartres, he offered abundant pearls of seemingly hidden wisdom, which were wrapped in metaphors, musings, and mischief. His stories—his magazine pieces, his books—offer timeless meditations on what humanity can really be, where it can end up, whether careful or not, and curiously, Hunter never seems to actually judge anyone, even when their actions *are* heinous.

Having had the good fortune to share time and space, among other delights, with Hunter a few times around twenty years ago in Los Angeles, I feel a few thoughts should be shared.

Firstly, his sense of observation, and both self-reflection and self-deprecation, were unlike any I had seen in anyone before . . . or after. In fact, he was everything you wanted him to be, including (and in no particular order):

A caricature of himself
Completely unfiltered
Unexpectedly fragile and human
Articulate

Blunt
Mildly offensive
Gentle
Somewhat aloof

And yes, I *genuinely* wanted him to be all of those things.

Above all, he was endlessly charismatic and magnetic. I'm hard pressed to think of anybody who drew you into his conscience so rapidly and immediately gave you the sense—just by being in the same space—of instantly viewing the world through his eyes. Was that him? His legend? The moment? All of it? None of it? Look, I don't know; all I can tell you is he was one very, very engaging motherfucker, while at the same time making everyone gathered feel unexpectedly safe and strangely at ease in such a tumultuous and contradictory element.

Everyone's been through some level of wringer these past few years. I wonder what Hunter would've made of it all. With the populists, the pandemic, and pockets of pandemonium

everywhere, he'd have been in there analyzing it all, delivering his dispatches from the front and center with no one safe from his vantage point on matters.

His reflections—and self-reflections—on what makes humanity tick and tock serve as great a purpose as ever in the chaos of today. These three stories—"Mescalito," "Death of a Poet," and "Screwjack"—remind us what a brilliant articulator Thompson was of the battle within a person's soul.

All that, and Hunter did it in a way that made you laugh your ass off and wanna jump screaming headfirst into the stories and join the shenanigans, just for the hell of it.

He was quite a guy . . .

April 2023

FOREWORD

Dear Maurice:

Hello. Have a nice day. Yes. *Mahalo.* Stand back. I have finally returned from the Wilderness, where I was chased & tormented by huge radioactive Bobcats for almost 22 weeks. When I finally escaped they put me in a Decompression Chamber with some people I couldn't recognize, so I went all to pieces & now I can't remember anything or Anybody or even *who I was,* all that time—which was exactly since *Groundhog Day,* when it started.

Anyway, that's why I fell behind in my correspondence for a while. *I could not be reached* except by the Animals, and they *hated* me. I never knew *Why.* There was no explanation for it.

* * *

So what? Who needs *reasons* for a thing like that? *Escape* is all that matters—except for the horrible scars, but that is a different question. Today we must deal with *The Book,* which requires my total attention *now.*

A brainless whore would not *say* this, Maurice. The Truth is not in them. But I am not a

brainless whore—and if I was, I don't remember it. Who cares? Shit happens. On some days I don't miss my memory at all. . . . Most days, in fact. It is like knowing that you were a Jackbastard in yr. Previous Life, then somebody tells you to be careful not to scream in yr. sleep anymore. You start to feel afraid. . . . But *not me*, Maurice.

As for the ORDER, I think *Screwjack* should be *last* & *Mescalito first*—so the dramatic tension (& also the true chronological weirdness) can *build* like *Bolero* to a faster & wilder climax that will drag the reader relentlessly *up* a hill, & then *drop* him off a cliff. . . . That is the Desired Effect, and if we *start* with *Screwjack* it won't happen. The book will peter out.

* * *

Okay. That's about it, for now. We can wrap this thing up very quickly, I think. . . . Indeed. And so much for all that. I have to go out in the yard to murder a skunk—and if I fail, he will murder *me*. Some things never change.

In closing, I remain—yr. calm & gentle friend,

Hunter

SCREWJACK

1

MESCALITO

Again in L.A., again at the Continental Hotel . . . full of pills and club sandwiches and Old Crow and now a fifth of Louis Martini Barbera, looking down from the eleventh floor balcony at a police ambulance screaming down toward the Whisky-a-Go-Go on the Strip, where I used to sit in the afternoon with Lionel and talk with off-duty hookers . . . and while I was standing there, watching four flower children in bell-bottom pants, two couples, hitch-hiking toward Holly-wood proper, a mile or so up the road . . . they noticed me looking down and waved. I waved, and moments later, after pointing me out to each other, they hoisted the "V" signal—and I returned that. And one of them yelled, "What are you doing up there?" And I said, "I'm writing about all you freaks down there on the street." We talked back and forth for a while, not communicating much, and I felt like Hubert Humphrey looking down at Grant Park. Maybe if Humphrey had had a balcony in that twenty-fifth-floor Hilton suite he might have behaved differently. Looking out a window is not quite the same. A balcony puts you out in the dark, which is more neutral—like walking out on a diving board. Anyway, I was struck by the distance between me and those street freaks; to them, I was just another fat cat, hanging off a balcony over the strip . . . and it reminded me of James Farmer on TV today, telling *Face the Nation* how he'd maintained his contacts with the Black Community, talking with fat jowls and a nervous hustler style, blundering along in the wake of George Herman's and Daniel Schorr's condescension . . . and then McGarr talking later, at the Luau, a Beverly Hills flesh pit, about how he could remember when Farmer was a radical and it scared him to see how far he'd drifted from the front lines . . . it scared him, he said, because he wondered if the same thing could happen to him . . . which gets back to my scene on the balcony—

Hubert Humphrey looking down at Grant Park on Tuesday night, when he still had options (then, moments later, the four flower children hailed a cab—yes, cab, taxi—and I walked down to the King's Cellar liquor store where the clerk looked at my Diners Club card and said, "Aren't you the guy who did that *Hell's Angels* thing?" And I felt redeemed. . . . Selah).

FEBRUARY 18

L.A. notes, again . . . one-thirty now and pill-fear grips the brain, staring down at this half-finished article . . . test pilots, after a week (no, three days) at Edwards AFB in the desert . . . but trying to mix writing and fucking around with old friends don't work no more, this maddening, time-killing late-work syndrome, never getting down to the real machine action until two or three at night, won't make it . . . especially half drunk full of pills and grass with deadlines past and people howling in New York . . . the pressure piles up like a hang-fire lightning ball in the brain. Tired and wiggy from no sleep or at least not enough.

Living on pills, phone calls unmade, people unseen, pages unwritten, money unmade, pressure piling up all around to make some kind of breakthrough and get moving again. Get the gum off the rails, finish something, croak this awful habit of not ever getting to the end—of anything.

And now the fire alarm goes off in the hall . . . terrible ringing of bells . . . but the hall is empty. Is the hotel on fire? Nobody answers the phone at the desk; the operator doesn't answer . . . the bell screams on. You read about hotel fires: 75 KILLED IN HOLOCAUST: LEAPING OFF BALCONIES (I am on the eleventh floor) . . . but apparently there is no fire. The operator finally answers and says a "wire got crossed." But nobody else is in the hall; this happened in Washington too, at the Nixon gig. False alarms and a man screaming down the airshaft, "Does anybody want to fuck?" The foundations are crumbling.

Yesterday a dope freak tried to steal the Goodyear blimp and take it to Aspen for the Rock and Roll festival . . . carrying a guitar and a toothbrush and a transistor radio he said was a bomb. . . . "Kept authorities at bay," said the L.A. *Times*, "for more than an hour, claiming to be George Harrison of the Beatles." They took him to jail but couldn't figure out what to charge him with . . . so they put him in a loony bin.

Meanwhile the hills keep crumbling, dropping houses down on streets and highways. Yesterday they closed two lanes of the Pacific Coast Highway between Sunset and Topanga . . . passing the scene in McGarr's little British-souvenir car on the way to Gover's house in Malibu . . . we looked up and saw two houses perched out in space, and dirt actually sliding down the cliff. It was only a matter of time, and no cure, no way to prevent these two houses from dropping on the highway. They keep undercutting the hills to make more house sites, and the hills keep falling. Fires burn the vegetation off in summer, rains make mud-slides in the winter . . . massive erosion, fire and mud, with The Earthquake scheduled for April. Nobody seems to give a fuck.

Today I found marijuana seeds all over the rug in my room . . . leaning down to tie my shoes I fo-

cused low and suddenly the rug was alive with seeds. Reminds me of the time I littered a hotel room in Missoula, Montana, with crab lice . . . picking them off, one by one, and hurling them around the room. . . . I was checking out for Butte. And also the last time I was in this hotel I had a shoe full of grass, and John Wilcock's package . . . awful scene at the Canadian border in Toronto, carrying all that grass and unable to say where I lived when they asked me. . . . I thought the end had come, but they let me through.

And now, by total accident, I find "Property of Fat City" (necessary cop-out change self-preservation—Oscar—looting) painted on the side of this borrowed typewriter. Is it stolen? God only knows . . . seeds on the rug and a hot typewriter on the desk, we live in a jungle of pending disasters, walking constantly across a minefield . . . will my plane crash tomorrow? What if I miss it? Will the next one crash? Will my house burn down? Gover's friend's house in Topanga burned yesterday, nothing saved except an original Cézanne. Where will it all end?

Getting toward dawn now, very foggy in the head . . . and no Dexedrine left. For the first time in at least five years I am out of my little energy bombs. Nothing in the bottle but five Ritalin tablets and a big spansule of mescaline and "speed." I don't know the ratio of the mixture, or what kind of speed is in there with the mescaline. I have no idea what it will do to my head, my heart, or my body. But the Ritalin is useless at this point—not strong enough—so I'll have to risk the other. Oscar is coming by at ten, to take me out to the airport for the flight to Denver and Aspen . . . so if I sink into madness and weird hallucinations, at least he can get me checked out of the hotel. The plane ride itself might be another matter. How can a man know? (Well, I just swallowed the bugger . . . soon it will take hold; I have no idea what to expect, and in this deadtired, run-down condition almost anything can happen. My resistance is gone, so any reaction will be extreme. I've never had mescaline.)

Meanwhile, outside on the Strip the zoo action never stops. For a while I watched four L.A. sheriffs beat up two teenagers, then handcuff them and haul them away. Terrible howls and screams floated up to my balcony. "I'm sorry, sir . . . Oh God, please, I'm sorry." WHACK. One cop picked him up by the feet while he was hanging on to a hurricane fence; the other one kicked him loose, then kneeled on his back and whacked him on the head a few times. I was tempted to hurl a wine bottle down on the cops but refrained. Later, more noise . . . this time a dope freak, bopping along and singing at the top of his lungs—some kind of medieval chant. Oblivious to everything, just bopping along the strip.

And remember that shooting scene in Alfie's . . . also the film opening with a man reeling into a plastic house, vomiting, cursing the news, picking up a pistol, and firing into the ceiling . . . driven mad by the news and the pressures of upward mobility . . . then, perhaps, to the Classic Cat on amateur night, his neighbor's wife . . .

and from there to the shooting at Alfie's . . . yes, it begins to jell.

Jesus, 6:45 now and the pill has taken hold for real. The metal on the typewriter has turned from dull green to a sort of high-gloss blue, the keys sparkle, glitter with highlights. . . . I sort of levitated in the chair, hovering in front of the typewriter, not sitting. Fantastic brightness on everything, polished and waxed with special lighting . . . and the physical end of the thing is like the first half-hour on acid, a sort of buzzing all over, a sense of being gripped by something, vibrating internally but with no outward sign or movement. I'm amazed that I can keep typing. I feel like both me and the typewriter have become weightless; it floats in front of me like a bright toy. Weird, I can still spell . . . but I had to think about that last one. . . . "Weird." Christ, I wonder how much worse this is going to get. It's seven now, and I have to check out in an hour or so. If this is the beginning of an acid-style trip I might as well give up on the idea of flying anywhere.

Taking off in an airplane right now would be an unbearable experience, it would blow the top right off my head. The physical sensations of lifting off the ground would be unbearable in this condition; I feel like I could step off the balcony right now and float gently down to the sidewalk. Yes, and getting worse, a muscle in my thigh is seized by spasms, quivering like something disembodied. . . . I can watch it, feel it, but not be connected. There is not much connection between my head and my body . . . but I can still type and very fast too, much faster than normal. Yes, the goddamn drug is definitely taking hold, very much like acid, a sense of very pleasant physical paralysis (wow, that spelling) while the brain copes with something never coped with before. The brain is doing all the work right now, adjusting to this new stimulus like an old soldier ambushed and panicked for a moment, getting a grip but not in command, hanging on, waiting for a break but expecting something worse . . . and yes, it's coming on. I couldn't possibly get out of this chair right now, I couldn't walk, all I can do is

∧∧∧∧∧∧∧∧∧∧∧∧∧∧∧∧

type . . . it feels like the blood is racing through me, all around my body, at fantastic speeds. I don't feel any pumping, just a sense of increased flow. . . . Speed. Interior speed . . . and a buzzing without noise, high-speed vibrations and more brightness. The little red indicator that moves along with the ball on this typewriter now appears to be made of arterial blood. It throbs and jumps along like a living thing.

I feel like vomiting, but the pressure is too great. My feet are cold, hands cold, head in a vise . . . fantastic effort to lift the bottle of Budweiser and take a sip, I drink like breathing it in, feeling it all the way cold into my stomach . . . very thirsty, but only a half a beer left and too early to call for more. Christ, there's the catch. I am going to have to deal with all manner of complicated shit like packing, paying, all that shit any moment now. If the thing bites down much harder I might wig out and demand beer . . . stay away from the phone, watch the red arrow . . . this typewriter is keeping me on my rails, without it I'd be completely adrift and weird. Maybe I should call Oscar and get him down here with some beer, to keep me away from that balcony. Ah shit, this is very weird, my legs are half frozen and a slow panic in my stomach, wondering how much stranger it will get . . . turn the radio on, focus on something but don't listen to the words, the vicious bullshit. . . . Jesus, the sun is coming up, the room is unbearably bright, then a cloud across the sun, I can see the cloud in the sudden loss of light in the room, now getting brighter as the cloud passes or moves . . . out there somewhere, much harder to type now, but it must be done, this is my handle, keep the brain tethered, hold it down. Any slippage now could be a landslide, losing the grip, falling or flipping around, Christ, can't blow my nose, can't find it but I can see it and my hand too, but they can't get together, ice in my nose, trembling with the radio on now, some kind of flute music, cold and fantastic vibration so fast I can't move . . . the ball just flipped back, a space capsule floating across the page, some kind of rotten phony soul music on the radio, Melvin Laird singing "The Weight" "O yes we get wearahe,

weeri, wearih?" Some fuckawful accent. Hair-
jelly music. Anthony Hatch in Jerusalem, great
God, the stinking news is on, get rid of it, no men-
tion of Nixon, too much for a tortured head. . . .
Christ, what a beastly job to look for a new station on this radio dial, up and down the bright
blue line and all these numbers, quick switch to
FM, get rid of the fucking news, find something
in a foreign language . . . the news is already on
the TV screen, but I won't turn it on, won't even
look at it. . . . Nixon's face. . . . GODDAMN, I
just called Oscar, fantastic effort to dial, and the
fucking line is busy . . . hang on now, no slippage,
ignore this weird trembling . . . laugh, yes, that
sense of humor, snag it down from somewhere,
the skyhook. . . . Jesus, I have to lock that door,
get the DO NOT DISTURB sign out before a maid
blunders in. I can't stand it, and I just heard one
out there, creeping along the hallway, jiggling
doorknobs . . . ho ho, yes, that famous smile . . .
yes, I just got hold of Oscar . . . he's coming with
some beer . . . that is the problem now, I can't
start fucking around with the management,

shouting for beer at this hour of dawn . . . disaster area that way, don't fuck with the management, not now in this wiggy condition . . . conserve this inch of beer until Oscar arrives with more, get a human buffer zone in here, something to hide behind . . . the fucking news is on again, on FM this time. Singer Sewing time is fifteen minutes until eight o'clock, Washington's Birthday sale we cannot tell a lie, our machines will sew you into a bag so fast you'll think you went blind . . . goddamn is there no human peaceful sound on the radio . . . yes, I had one for an instant, but now more ads and bullshit . . . now, right there, a violin sound, hold that, stay with it, focus on that violin sound, ride it out . . . ah, this beer won't last, the thirst will doom me to fucking with the management . . . no, I have some ice left—on the balcony—but careful out there, don't look over the edge . . . go out backward, feel around for the paper ice bucket, seize it carefully between thumb and forefinger, then walk slowly back to this chair . . . try it now. . . . DONE, but my legs have turned to jelly, impossible to move around except like a rolling ball, don't bounce, get away from that phone, keep typing, the grip, the handle. . . . Jesus, my hands are vibrating now, I don't see how they can type. The keys feel like huge plastic mounds, very mushy and that bright red arrow jumping along like a pill in one of those sing-along movie shorts, bouncing from word to word with the music. . . . Thank God for the *Sonata in F Major for Oboe and Guitar* by Charles Starkweather . . . no ads, listener-sponsored radio, not even news . . . salvation has many faces, remind me to send a check to this station when I get well . . . KPFK? Sounds right. The beer crisis is building, I am down to saliva in this last brown bottle . . . goddamn, half my brain is already pondering how to get more beer, but it won't work . . . no way. No beer is available here. No way. Nao tem. Think about something else, thank God for this music; if I could get to the bathroom I'd like to get a towel and hang it over the face of this stinking TV set, the news is on there, I can smell it. My eyes feel bigger than grapefruits. Where are the sunglasses,

I see them over there, creep across, that cloud is off the sun again, for real this time, incredible light in the room, white blaze on the walls, glittering typewriter keys . . . and down there under the balcony traffic moves steadily along the Sunset Strip in Hollywood, California, zip code unknown . . . we just came back from a tour of the Soviet Union and Denmark, careful now, don't stray into the news, keep it pure, yes, I hear a flute now, music starting again. What about cigarettes, another problem area . . . and I hear that wily old charwoman sucking on the doorknob again, goddamn her sneaky ass what does she want? I have no money. If she comes in here the rest of her days will be spent in a fear-coma. I am not in the mood to fuck around with charwomen, keep them out of here, they prowl this hotel like crippled wolves . . . smile again, yes, gain a step, tighten the grip, ho ho. . . . When will this thing peak? It seems to be boring deeper. I know it can't be worse than acid, but that's what it feels like now. I have to catch a plane in two hours. Can it be done? Jesus, I couldn't fly now. . . . I couldn't walk to the plane . . . oh Jesus, the crunch is on, my throat and mouth are like hot gravel and even the saliva is gone . . . can I get to the bottle of Old Crow and mix it up with the remains of these ice fragments . . . a cool drink for the freak? Give the gentleman something cool, dear, can't you see he's wired his brain to the water pump and his ears to the generator . . . stand back, those sparks! Back off, maybe he's too far gone . . . coil a snake around him . . . get that drink, boy, you are slipping, we need CONCENTRATION . . . yes, the music, some kind of German flower song. Martin Bormann sings WHITE RABBIT . . . ambushed in the jungle by a legion of naked gooks . . . whiskey uber alles, get that drink, get up, move.

DONE . . . but my knees are locked and my head is about twenty feet higher than my feet . . . in this room with an eight-foot roof, making travel very difficult. The light again, get those sunglasses, unlock the knees and creep over there . . . not far . . . yes, I'm wearing the glasses now, but the glare is still all around. Getting out of this hotel and catching this plane is going to be weird. . . . I see not much hope, but that's not the way to think. . . . I have managed to do everything else I've had to do so far. Twenty-three minutes past eight on this brain-saving station, I hear echoes of the news, leaking out the back of the TV set. . . . Nixon has ordered the Condor Legion into Berkeley . . . smile . . . relax a bit, sip that drink. Bagpipes now on the radio, but it's really violins . . . they're fucking around with these instruments, sounds like a tractor in the hall, the charwomen are going to cave my door in with a fucking webbed vehicle, a crane in the hall, snapping doors off their hinges like so many cobwebs . . . creaking and clanking along, this hotel has gone all to hell since the chain took it over, no more grapefruit in the light sockets, the lamp sockets . . . put some lampblack on these walls, take off the glare. We need more hair on these walls, and crab lice in the rug to give it life. There are marijuana seeds in this rug, the place is full of them. The rug crackles like popcorn when I walk, who planted these seeds in this rug, and why aren't they watered? Now . . . yes . . . there is a project, tend the crops, soak this rug like a drenching rain, some kind of tropical downpour . . . good for the crops, keep the ground damp and prune the leaves every other day. Be careful about renting the room, special people, nature freaks, tillers of the soil . . . let them in, but for Christ's sake keep the charwomen out. They don't like things growing in the rug, most of them seem like third-generation Finns, old muscles turned to lard and hanging like wasps nests. . . .

Wasps nests? Slipping again, beware, Oscar just came in, bringing beer. I seem to have leveled out, like after the first rush of acid. If this is as deep as it's going to bore I think we can make that plane, but I dread it. Getting in a steel tube and shot across the sky, strapped down . . . yes, I sense a peak, just now, a hint of letdown, but still vibrating and hovering around with the typewriter. The cloud is over the sun again, or maybe it's smog . . . but the glare is gone from the walls, no highlights on the buildings down below, no sparkle on the rooftops, no water, just gray air. I see a concrete mixer moving, red and gray, down on that other street a long way off. It looks like a Matchbox toy; they sell them in airports. Get one for Juan. I think we will catch that plane. Some-day when things are right and like they should be we can do all this again by putting a quarter in the Holiday Inn vibrator bed and taking a special madness pill . . . but wait, hold over there, we can do *that* now. We can do almost anything now . . . and why not?

* * *

Xerox copy with author's notes of yesterday's program for today's Continental Airlines tape con-cert—private earphones for all passengers and six-channel selector dials, along with individual volume controls, built into each seat. The "pro-gram" being twenty-four hours old plays hell with a head full of cactus madness—like watch-ing an NFL football game with an AFL roster.

* * *

11:32—hovering again. Weightless—weird—L.A. down below—earphones and knobs—switching around Jesus, Leon Blum—the Canadian Legion Haile Selassie speech.

* * *

Cheap rental cars at the airport—seize Batrollers and zang up to Big Sur—have Michael Murphy arrested for restraint of trade, killing the last true hillbilly-music cabal on the West Coast. Who can blame me for whipping on that paraplegic in the baths? Anyone would have done it—Selah.

* * *

Who are these pigs—as a validated addict I demand to be left alone—drink the eucalyptus oil—with dials and knobs still high as a freak male locked into the vibrations of the jet engines—get a bag of acid and a credit card for airlines—evaluate the pitch, roll and yaw—no sense of movement in this plane—just humming—the phones—acid-style high tingling and strange, intense vibrations. Get that dead animal off the seat—put it under—where is the drink? These pigs are taking us for a ride—put it on the card. Strange feedback echoes on the headset, Gabriel Heatter screaming in the background—telephone conversations—fantastic people talking. This is yesterday's program—new songs today. A dingbat across the aisle and Kitty Wells on the headphones. This channel is hag-ridden with echoes—telephone conversations. See no wings on this plane—good God the lock on my whiskey bag is frozen—a lifting body, tends to destroy itself, very wormy. I seem to be getting higher. (12:15.) Warn the pilot—this plane feels very wormy at this altitude. An ominous sense of yaw . . . sliding off edge—fire in the ashtray. Weird things in this channel.

* * *

Further notes in the Denver airport—coming down but can't relax, looking for a plane ride to Aspen with all legitimate flights canceled due to snowstorm—if not to Aspen, then back to L.A.— last chance to get straight—final effort—and half wanting the abyss. One of you pigs will find me a plane—sweating obscenely, hair plastered down and dripping from the cheekbones—the drug is gone now, no more zang, failing energy, disconnected thoughts—the Goodyear blimp as a last resort but no driving. Beware of (unreadable) hawks in the company of straight people—get that charter, leaving in five minutes—fiery stom-ach, running through the airport screaming for Bromo-Seltzer—coming down again in the Denver airport. Now, sitting in the copilot's seat of an Aero Commander—weirdness feeds on itself—with a wheel in my lap and pedals on the floor at my feet—forty-one round dials in front of me, blinking lights, jabbering radio noise—smoking, waiting for the oxygen—sick, feeling deranged—two Ritalins don't help much—sliding—no hope of pulling out—air bubbles in the brain—open this window beside me, a rush of air and crisis sounds from the others. Smelling of booze in this tiny cabin, nobody speaks—fear and loathing, dizzy, flying and bouncing through clouds. No more hole-cards, drained. Back to L.A., rather than Grand Junction—why go there? Chaos in the Denver airport—soaking sweats and all flights canceled—charwomen working—lying swine at the counters—"here boy, rent this car." Sorry, as a certified addict I cannot drive on snow—I must fly!

LOS ANGELES, 1969

DEATH OF A POET

In the coffin of ice, I sleep naked
In the tunnel of fire, I drink
—F. X. LEACH

It was dark when we dropped into Green Bay, and the airport was deadly calm. The whole town was in shock from the disastrous beating inflicted that day on the hometown Packers by the Kansas City Chiefs. . . . Their confidence was broken; the Magic Man had failed, Mighty Casey had struck out.

The girl at the Avis counter was weeping uncontrollably in her booth as I approached. My heart was filled with joy, but I couldn't get through to her. She had lost her will to live. "Take any car you want," she said. "I don't care anymore: It's over. I'm moving to Milwaukee on Monday."

"Who cares?" I said. "Give me some goddamn keys." She was slow to respond so I gave her a taste of the long knuckle and she fell to her knees. "There's more where that came from," I told her.

Then I grabbed a set of keys off a nail and hur-

43

∧∧∧∧∧∧∧∧∧∧∧∧∧∧∧∧∧

ried outside to find a car. I was eager to see Leach and celebrate our great victory.

* * *

The address he had given me turned out to be a trailer court behind the stockyards. He met me at the door with red eyes and trembling hands, wearing a soiled cowhide bathrobe and carrying a half-gallon of Wild Turkey.

"You got here just in time," he said. "I was about to slit my wrists. This is the worst day of my life."

"Nonsense," I said. "We won big. I bet the same way you did. You gave me the numbers. You even predicted Kansas City would stomp the Packers."

F.X. tensed, then he threw back his head and uttered a high-pitch quavering shriek. I seized him. "Get a grip on yourself," I snapped. "What's wrong?"

"I went crazy," he said. "I got drunk and changed my bet. Then I doubled up."

I felt a shudder in my spine. "What!" I said. "You bet on the Packers? What happened?"

"I went to that big Packer pep rally with some guys from the shop," he said. "We were all drinking schnapps and screaming and I lost my head. . . . It was impossible to bet against the Packers in that atmosphere."

It was true. Leach was a bad drinker and a junkie for mass hysteria.

"They're going to kill me," he said. "They'll be here by midnight. I'm doomed." He uttered another low cry and reached for the Wild Turkey bottle, which had fallen over and spilled.

"Hang on," I said. "I'll get more."

On my way to the kitchen I was jolted by the sight of a naked woman slumped awkwardly in the corner with a desperate look on her face, as if she'd been shot. Her eyes were bulged and her mouth was wide open and she appeared to be reaching out for me.

I leaped back and heard laughter behind me. My first thought was that Leach, unhinged by his gambling disaster, had finally gone over the line with his wife-beating habit and shot her in the mouth just before I knocked on the door. She appeared to be crying out for help, but there was no voice.

I ran into the kitchen and looked around for a knife thinking that if Leach had gone crazy enough to kill his wife, now he would have to kill me too, since I was the only witness.

Suddenly he appeared in the doorway, holding the naked woman by the neck, and hurled her across the room at me. . . .

. . . Time stood still for an instant. The woman seemed to hover in the air, coming at me in the darkness like a body in slow motion. I went into a stance with the bread knife and braced for fighting.

Then the thing hit me and bounced softly down to the floor. It was a rubber blow-up doll: one of those things with five orifices that young stockbrokers buy in adult bookstores after the singles bars close.

"Meet Jennifer," he said. "She's my punching bag." He picked up the doll by her hair and slammed it across the room.

"Ho,ho," he chuckled. "No more wife beat-

ing. I'm cured, thanks to Jennifer." He smiled
sheepishly. "It's almost like a miracle. These dolls
saved my marriage. They're a lot smarter than you
think," he nodded gravely. "Sometimes I have to
beat two at once, but it always calms me down,
you know what I mean?"

Whoops, I thought. Welcome to the night
train. "Oh hell yes," I said quickly. "How do the
neighbors handle it?"

"No problem," he said. "They love me."

Sure, I thought. I tried to imagine the horror
of living in a muddy industrial lot full of tin-
walled trailers and trying to protect your family
against brain damage from knowing that, every
night when you look out your kitchen to check
out the neighbor's unit, there will be a man in a
leather bathrobe flogging two naked women
around the room with a quart of Wild Turkey.
Sometimes for two or three hours. . . . It was horrible.

"How is your wife?" I asked. "Is she still
here?"

"Oh yes," he said quickly. "She just went out

for some cigarettes. She'll be back any minute." He nodded eagerly. "Oh yes, she's very proud of me. We're almost reconciled. She really loves these dolls."

I smiled, but something about his story made me nervous. "How many do you have?" I asked him.

"Don't worry," he said. "I have all we need." He reached into a nearby broom closet and pulled out another one, a half-inflated Chinese-looking woman with rings in her nipples and two electric cords attached to her head. "This is Ling-Ling," he said. "Screams when I hit her." He whacked the doll's head and it squawked stupidly.

Just then we heard car doors slamming outside the trailer, a loud knocking on the front door and a gruff voice shouting, "Open up! Police!"

Leach grabbed a snub-nosed .44 Magnum out of a shoulder holster inside his bathrobe and fired two shots through the front door. "You bitch," he screamed. "I should have killed you a long time ago."

He fired two more shots, laughing calmly.

Then he turned to face me and put the barrel of the gun in his mouth. He hesitated for a moment, staring directly into my eyes. Then he pulled the trigger and blew off the back of his head.

3

SCREWJACK

Among the many documents, manuscripts, personal papers and artworks that miraculously survived the Great Firestorm that swept the Duke Estate in the winter of '88 was this one—a profoundly disturbing love letter that he wrote to his wife only sixteen days before his disappearance.

The first few lines contain no warning of the madness and fear and lust that came more and more to plague him and dominate his life, as he felt his crimes coming back to haunt him.

—THE EDITORS

I was just joined by the rich and famous Mr. Screwjack, who ate the last of the tuna fish and gave me one of those head jobs under the chin, and then tried to coax me outside with him, but I refused . . . so he shrugged and went out by himself, into the cold and sunless dawn.

He would rather have stayed inside with me—the two of us curled up on the couch together, watching Oprah Winfrey on TV . . . I could see it in his cold yellow eyes, a wistful kind of yearning for love that would have to wait, or perhaps could never be. . . .

53

His whining drove me crazy as I carried him in my arms to the front door and just before I hurled his wretched black ass out onto the thin crust of snow that had settled on the porch since midnight, I lifted him up to my face and kissed him deeply on the lips. I forced my tongue between his fangs and rolled it around the ridges on the top of his mouth. I gripped him around his strong young shoulders and pulled him closer to me. His purring was so loud and strong that it made us both tremble.

"Ah, sweet Screwjack," I whispered. "We are doomed. Mama has gone off to Real Estate School and then to El Centro, and after that maybe even to Law School. We will never see her again."

He stared at me, but said nothing. Then he twisted out of my grip and dropped to the floor. . . . And then he was gone, with no noise, like some ghost from my other world . . . and I knew in my heart, as his dirty black shape leaped away from me across the woodpile and through that shadowy hole between the blue spruce tree and

the cold silver grille of the Volvo, that I would never see him again.

At least not for six years, and probably not then; and the next time we met he would weigh 200 pounds and flip me over on my stomach and fuck me from behind like a panther.

Like my beast and my dolphin, my perfect dream lover, like that ghost that I must forget . . . and my beautiful little tattoo that will cost me $1500 to get burned off my shoulder with a laser needle.

Forgive me Lord, for loving this beast like I do, and for wanting him so deep inside me that I will finally feel him coming on the soft red skin of my own heart . . . and for wanting to lay down beside him and sleep like a baby with our bodies wrapped into each other and the same wild dream in our heads.

I am guilty, Lord, but I am also a lover—and I am one of your best people, as you know; and yea tho I have walked in many strange shadows and acted crazy from time to time and even drooled on many High Priests, I have not been an embarrassment to you. . . . So leave me alone, goddamnit, and send Mr. Screwjack back to me; and if the others have any questions or snide comments about it, tell them to eat shit and die.

Who among them is pure enough to cast the first stone? Or to look on me with those rheumy courtroom eyes and say that I was wrong for loving a huge black tomcat.

Never mind that, Lord. I can handle it. Just keep the lawyers off my back, and the pious . . . and leave us alone to make babies.

R.D.

At the depths of my social leperism I remember Duke's strange letter. . . . And I am horrified to realize that I am fondling the cat. . . . We were smoking marijuana a moment ago, maybe for one or two minutes, and now he is acting wild. He is rolling his nuts at me *for real* this time, on his back in my lap and suddenly curling up to put his fangs on me. He uttered a low kind of whimpering sound, then he opened his mouth and grabbed

the ball-muscle of my right thumb with all four of those goddamn white fangs (I was stroking his navel, at the time) . . . and for one very high tenth of a second I thought the crazy black bastard was going to do it.

I was typing, but once The Boy put his fangs on me, things changed. I stared down at him very intently from a distance of five or six inches (compounded by a factor of 1.25 by the specs). . . . So I felt pretty close to the beast when he suddenly curled up in my lap and began sinking his teeth into me.

That's how it felt. It was a very interesting sensation, because I believed it was really happening. This monster was actually going to *puncture* me, draw *blood*, and change our lives forever.

Goddamnit! I thought. You fool! I trusted you, but I was wrong. You're no better than that punk Mailer fell for . . . and now I *must* cut your head off. . . . And then the beast said "nevermore."

It was a very long moment, no more than a second—and then he suddenly relaxed and rolled his head back, releasing his bite on my thumb-muscle, as if it had never happened. . . . He pushed his wiry little neck back against the palm of my left hand and gazed up at me.

I closed my fingers around his neck and got a firm grip on his shoulders. He began to purr and the pupils in his eyes closed down to blissful little black slits as he wantonly ground his sharp, ugly little hipbones down into the palm of my right hand, the one he almost bit.

The phone rang. It was Pat Caddell, calling from Santa Barbara with a whole raft of ugly political news. "I can't talk now," I said. "I have to deal with this animal. Call me back when you calm down."

Then I hung up the phone and looked down, once again, at Screwjack. "You're lucky," I told him. "That was Mr. Caddell, the political man. He sends you his best regards."

Then I clamped my fingers very suddenly around his neck in a vise-like grip that cut his wind off, while at the same time dragging his head backward and straight down, over my leg, causing his front claws to flap crazily in the air as he struggled. . . .

With my right hand I seized the whole lower end of his body, between the front side of his groin and on the back where the tail connects to the spine, and I squeezed him like a grape.

There was no noise. He was bent and stretched out so far that he couldn't even hiss. . . . But not for long; it was a matter of split seconds before he was up in the air like a fruit bat, and then down into a trembling four-point stance about ten feet across the room. His eyes were huge and his white fangs were out of his mouth.

"What's wrong?" I asked him. "Why are you staring at me like that?" He shuddered and sat down heavily on the floor, near the icebox, saying nothing.

Hunter S. Thompson was born and raised in Louisville, Kentucky. His books include *Hell's Angels*, *Fear and Loathing in Las Vegas*, and *Fear and Loathing at Rolling Stone*. He died in 2005.